l a u r e n   c h i l d

I am TOO absolutely small for school

featuring **Charlie** and **Lola**

TED SMART

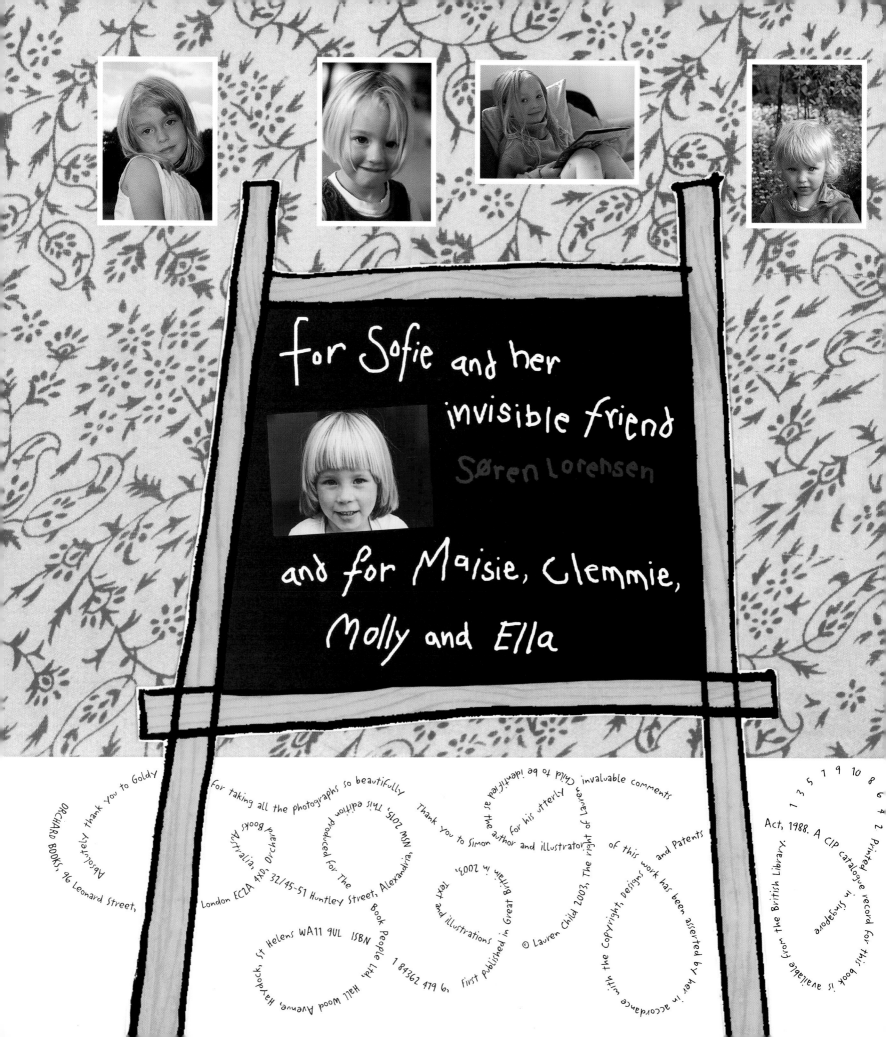

for Sofie and her invisible friend Søren Lorensen

and for Maisie, Clemmie, Molly and Ella

Absolutely thank you to Goldy for taking all the photographs so beautifully

ORCHARD BOOKS, 96 Leonard Street, London EC2A 4XD, Orchard Books Australia, 32/45-51 Huntley Street, Alexandria, NSW 2015. This edition produced for The Book People Ltd, Hall Wood Avenue, Haydock, St Helens WA11 9UL ISBN 1 84362 479 6, First published in Great Britain in 2003. Text and illustrations © Lauren Child 2003, The right of Lauren Child to be identified as the author and illustrator for his utterly invaluable comments of this work has been asserted by her in accordance with the Copyright, Designs and Patents Act, 1988. A CIP catalogue record for this book is available from the British Library.

Thank you to Simon

Printed in Singapore

1 3 5 7 9 10 8 6 4 2

I have this little
sister Lola.
She is small
and very funny.

Now Mum and Dad
say she is nearly
quite big enough
to go to school.

Lola is not
so sure.

huge

giantish

big

biggish

smallish

slightly small

small

tiny

teeny

titchy

Lola

says,

"I am **absolutely** not **BIG.**

I am still

really quite small."

Charlie

She says,

"I probably do not have **time** to go to school. I am too **extremely busy** doing **important things** at **home**."

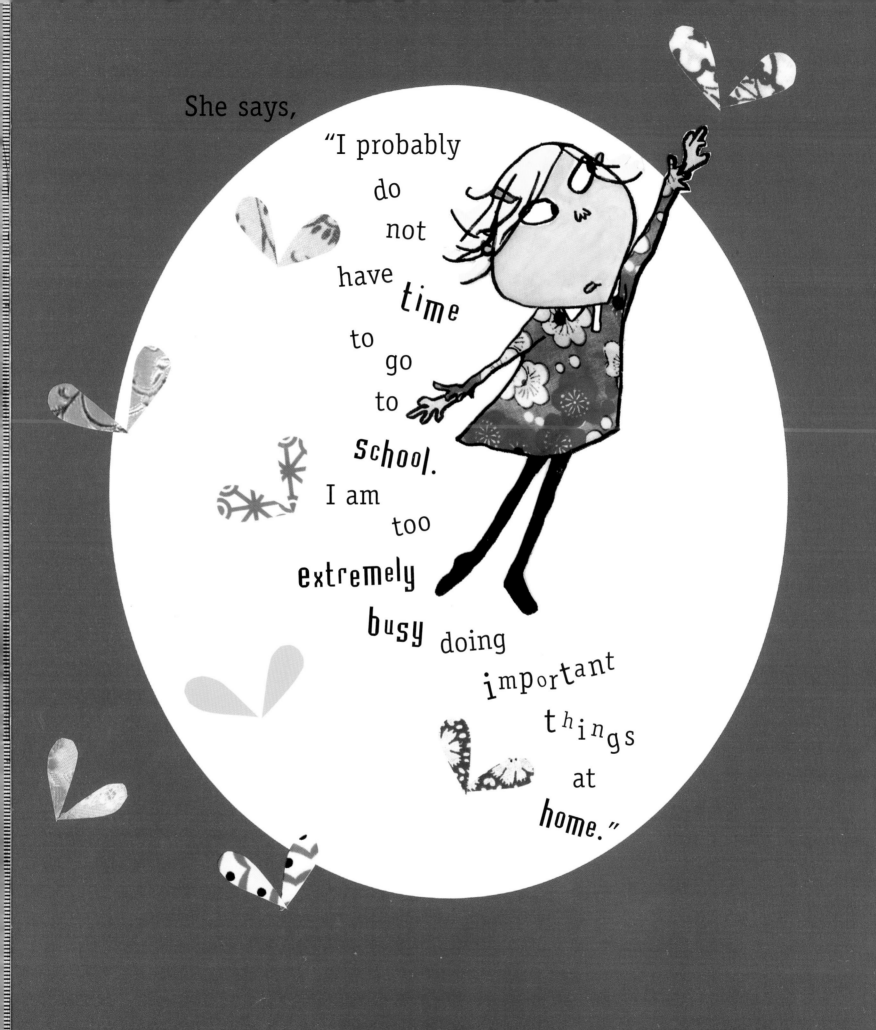

I say,
"At school
you will learn
numbers and how to
count up to one hundred."

Lola says,
"I don't need to
learn up to one hundred.
I already know up to ten
and that is plenty.

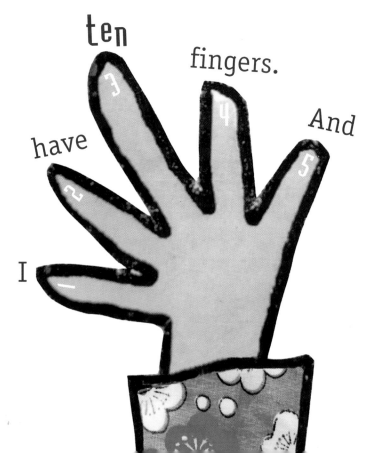

I have ten fingers.

And also I have ten toes.

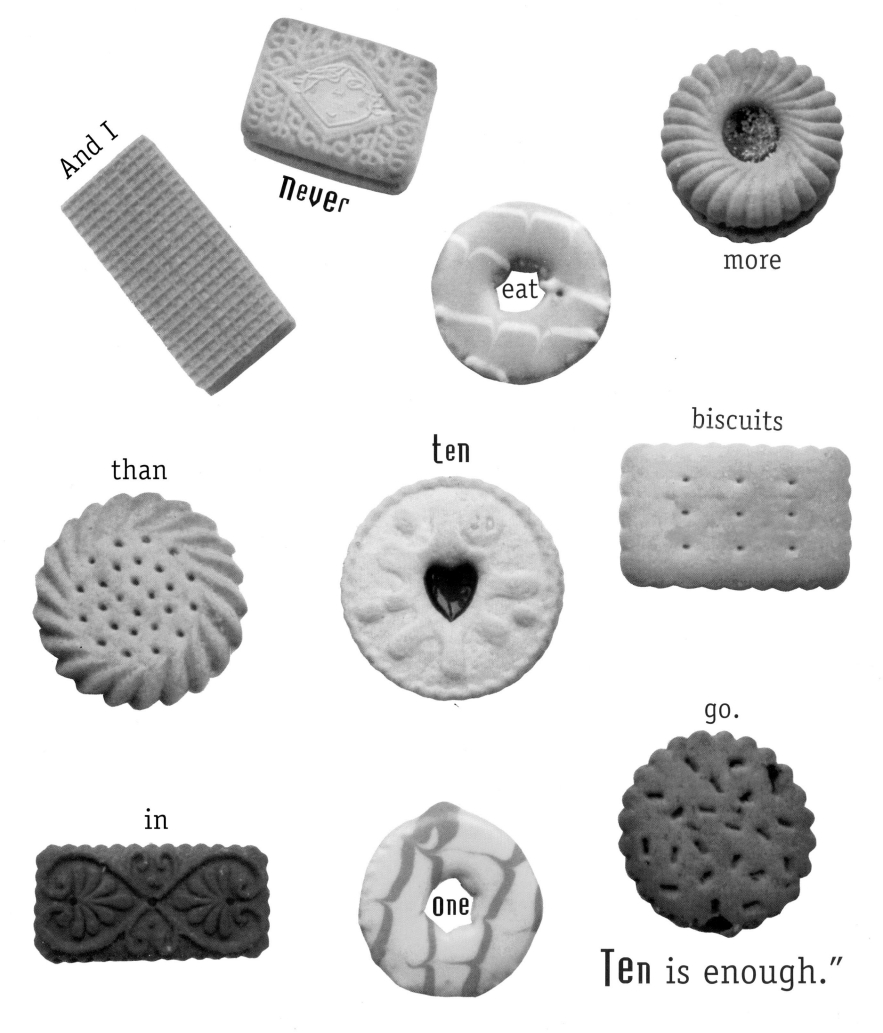

And I

Never

more

eat

than

ten

biscuits

go.

in

One

Ten is enough."

"But Lola," I say, "what if eleven eager elephants all wanted a treat.

How would you count up how many treats that would be?"

"Well," says Lola.

"I am not quite sure."

I say,

"And what about learning your

letters, Lola?

If you know how to write,

you can send cards to

people you like. "

Lola says,
"I like to talk on the telephone, it's more friendly and straightaway."

"But not everyone has a telephone you know," Lola," I say.

"Who doesn't?" says Lola.

"Father Christmas," I say. "You have to write him a special note and put it up the chimney to tell his little helpers your Christmas wish. Otherwise the little helpers might get your wish muddled up."

"I didn't know
that, Charlie,"
says Lola.

"And Lola," I say,
    "don't you want to
read words? Then you will
        be able to **read** your
own **books.** And understand
secret messages written
on the fridge."

Lola says,
    "I know lots of **secrets.**
I don't need to **read words,**
        and I've got all my
books in my head.
    If I can't remember, I
can just make them up."

"But Lola," I say, "what would you do if there was an ever so angry ogre who would not go to sleep unless you read him his favourite bedtime story?"

"I don't know, Charlie,"

says Lola.

Then Lola says,
    "I **would** like to
read to an ogre and
    count up elephants and
put **notes** up the chimbley.
But I **absolutely** will NOT
    ever wear a **schooliform**.
I do not like wearing the
same as other people."

I say,
    "But Lola, you do
not have to wear a
    school uniform. At our
school you can wear
    whatever you like."

"**Oh**," says Lola.
    "You wait there. I know
exactly what I can wear..."

"Well, Lola," I say,
        "that certainly suits you,

                but you **cannot** go to school
        dressed as a **crocodile**."

Lola says,
        "This is **not** a **crocodile**, this is a **alligator**."

I say, "You can't really go
                as an **alligator** either."

"Why
not?"
says
Lola.

charlie

"I like to wear stripes," says Lola, "but what will I do at lunchtime? You know I will NOT ever never eat a school dinner." My sister Lola is fussy about food.

I say, "But Lola, you can take your very own packed lunch in your very own lunch box."

Lola says, "I do not want to eat at school, **alone**, all by myself on my own."

I say, "But Lola, at school you will meet lots of new **friends**. You can have **lunch** with one of them."

Then Lola says, "But I already have **my friend** Soren Lorensen. I would like to have **lunch** at **home** with him."

Soren Lorensen is Lola's invisible friend. No one knows what he looks like.

"Oh you're right. Soren Lorensen is a bit slightly **nervous** to be at school on his **own**.

I will **absolutely** have to go **too**," says Lola.

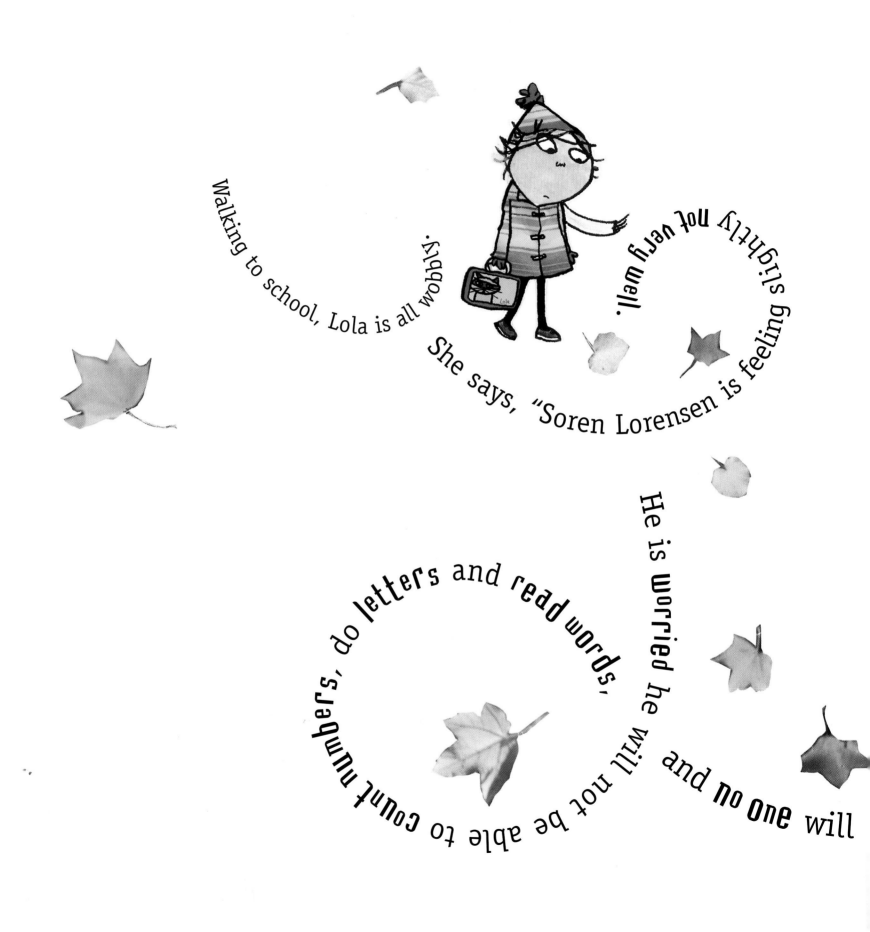

Walking to school, Lola is all wobbly.

She says, "Soren Lorensen is feeling slightly not very well.

He is worried he will not be able to count numbers, do letters and read words, and no one will

"Lola," I say, "it will be OK. You'll be fine. I bet you'll both have a really good time. And after school we'll have pink milk at home."

talk to him so he will be all by himself on his own."

But all day I am **worried.**

I don't see her at break,

and she's nowhere at lunch.

At home, I say,
    "Lola, I **told you** that you would
        have a **good time.**"
And Lola says,
    "Oh I know Charlie, I was not
worried. It was Soren Lorensen
        who was nervous, **not me.**
    I was **fine.**"